SPEARMINT FARM

PAPER COMPANY

ROUND-HOUSE

CELERY FIELDS

KALAMAZOO COLLEGE

KALAMAZOO

MATTAWAN

LAWTON

GRAPE JUICE PLANT

VINEYARDS

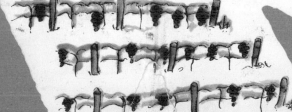

WESTERN MICHIGAN COLLEGE

History

The Fruit Belt Train was originally known as the Toledo and South Haven Railroad and was opened in 1877. At this time this railroad ran from South Haven, Michigan, and passed through the towns of Hartford, Lawrence, Paw Paw and Lawton, Michigan, and on to Toledo, Ohio.

Later, in 1903, the South Haven and Eastern Railroad was taken over by the Pere Marquette Railroad and a spur was laid from Paw Paw to Kalamazoo, Michigan.

Therefore, the Fruit Belt Train as this author remembers it ran from Kalamazoo to South Haven. It is interesting to note that the original road bed paralleled what is now the Michigan-Central and can be seen today as one leaves Kalamazoo for Chicago. Now, most of the track is gone— only the road bed remains of what was once a fascinating sight . . .

"The Fruit Belt Train"

To Lonnie Richard

The Engine
That Lost Its Whistle

The Fruit Belt Train—1877

jC8838e

Story and Pictures by Genevieve Cross

CROSS PUBLICATIONS

NEW YORK — KANSAS CITY

NOT so very long ago, and this was in Michigan, a little steam train puffed its way along a bumpy track that ran in and out the grape-vines, the peach trees, the cherry trees and the apple orchards.

Because this little train carried so much fruit on its way up and down the track each day, it was called, "The Fruit Belt Train," with a very proud engine named "Engine Number Seven."

EACH day Engine Number Seven steamed and steamed as he waited for the people to say good-bye and hurry into the coaches.

Each day Engine Number Seven blew his whistle loudly and puffed proudly away from the station as much as to say,

"I'm the biggest,
I'm the fastest engine on this track.
Watch me run!"

THAT was just what the country folks did. When it was time for Engine Number Seven to come snorting down the wobbley track, they stood by the fences to watch him run by. So did the cows with their new baby calves. But the horses — they ran away kicking their heels as frightened as they could be at big Engine Number Seven.

THIS pleased Engine Number Seven and made him run faster. Faster and faster he ran . . . that is . . . until he began to climb Allen's High Hill. Then he began to go slower, for Allen's High Hill was also a very long hill and he almost always had to stop half way up and let part of the cars roll back down.

SO that was what happened this time. He pulled part of the cars to the top of the hill and then came back for the rest. When he had them at the top of the hill he ran around and gave them one *BIG BUMP!*

WITH a sudden jerk the train began to move forward over the hill, slowly at first, and then a little faster. Faster, then faster, until it seemed to the people in the coaches that Engine Number Seven must be running away.

But Engine Number Seven only swayed from side to side and ran wildly on, laughing as he ran.

NOW it so happened that every night a Little Switch Engine stood next to Engine Number Seven and listened to all the exciting stories which Engine Number Seven told about his trips through the Fruit Country.

All these stories made Little Switch Engine very sad . . . sad . . . because he knew he never could pull people wildly through the air and frighten the horses with his whistle, nor could he run fast like Engine Number Seven, for his wheels were much too small. All he could ever hope to do was pull freight cars around the yards and once in a long time take the brakeman for a ride on his front step.

ONE night, Sleepy Engine Number Seven heard a soft voice whisper, "Engine Number Seven, will you take me with you to see all those people . . . and the horses . . . kicking their heels?"

"Take you with me," sighed Engine Number Seven. "I'll never take you with me for I'll never need you. You are only a Switch Engine. You belong here in the yards. You couldn't possibly pull the cars as fast as I can."

Then he closed his eyes . . . gave one last puff of smoke . . . then went quickly to sleep.

All night long, sad Little Switch Engine thought, "Why, oh, why, must I be only a Switch Engine? Why, oh why?"

THE next day, Engine Number Seven awoke as his big round sides began to fill with steam. Soon he was ready to start his trip through the fruit country. As always, he forgot all about the Little Switch Engine, who had been hard at work in the yards since early morning. Instead, all he thought was, "I wonder how many people will be waiting to see me today? Today, I will run my fastest."

Well, that was just what Engine Number Seven did. He steamed until his sides almost burst and he puffed his biggest puffs of smoke — and this day he carried all the people and all the cars over Allen's High Hill at one time!

As he started down the hill he thought, "Now, won't I have something to tell Little Switch Engine tonight!" Then he began to run fast.

SOON Engine Number Seven was running very fast . . . so fast, he had to hug the tracks to keep his big wheels from jumping off! He raced by the people, the cows and the calves, and sent the horses galloping across the field.

"Stop! . . . Stop!" shouted the people. But all they heard was —

"Toot! - Toot!
Get out of my way
I'm running my very
Fastest today."

Then they heard —

"Toot! - Toot! - SH - Sh - sh - sh - oo - oo"

AT once, Engine Number Seven began to slow up. Slower and slower he went. The people looked out of the windows. They wondered, "What is happening to Engine Number Seven? Why is he stopping?"

Soon they knew, for Engine Number Seven stopped still and looked about him. Water was dropping down his big round sides.

Poor Engine Number Seven! He had lost all his steam . . . because he had lost his Whistle!

Now he could not move. All he could do was wait for someone to come and help him.

Poor Engine Number Seven!

SOON someone did. And much to his surprise, it was the Little Switch Engine not sad at all, but looking bigger and stronger than Engine Number Seven had ever seen him look.

Quickly, Little Switch Engine gave him one big bump, and began pulling the train of cars down the track towards home.

As Little Switch Engine proudly puffed along, Engine Number Seven was sure he heard not a soft voice, but a strong voice chugging,

"I can do it

I can do it

I can do it too.

Even if I'm

Even if I'm

Not as big as you."

"So you can," said Engine Number Seven, loudly enough for Little Switch Engine to hear him.

Then he turned to look for his lost whistle!

The End

VAN BUREN COUNTY
FAIR GROUNDS

FREE Welcome FAIR

CHERRY ORCHARDS

INDIAN RESERVATION

To
SOUTH
HAVEN

HARTFORD

LAWRENCE

ALLEN'S HIGH HILL

WARING'S
COTTAGE

REYNOLDS
LAKE

CRISTY
LAKE

APPLE ORCHARDS
CANNING
FACTORY